MARY ENGELBREIT'S MOTHER GOOSE

MARY ENGELBREIT'S MOTHER GOOSE

ONE HUNDRED BEST-LOVED VERSES

With an Introduction by
LEONARD S. MARCUS

HARPERCOLLINS*PUBLISHERS*

I would like to thank the many folks at Mary Engelbreit Studios who helped make it possible for me to bring my vision of Mother Goose to life, including Jen, Dave, Pam, Wende, Jackie, Casey, and Alexa. I would especially like to thank Stephanie Barken, whose creative organization makes my life so much easier.

Leonard S. Marcus is one of the children's book world's most respected historians and critics. His books include *Margaret Wise Brown: Awakened by the Moon*; *Dear Genius: The Letters of Ursula Nordstrom*; *Ways of Telling*; and *Storied City*.

Mary Engelbreit's Mother Goose
Collection and illustrations copyright © 2005 by Mary Engelbreit Ink
Introduction copyright © 2005 by Leonard S. Marcus
Manufactured in China.
All rights reserved.
www.harperchildrens.com

Library of Congress Cataloging-in-Publication Data
Engelbreit, Mary.
Mary Engelbreit's Mother Goose : one hundred best-loved verses.
p.   cm.
Summary: An illustrated collection of one hundred nursery rhymes, including "Twinkle, Twinkle Little Star" and other familiar poems, as well as "Mary Had a Pretty Bird" and other less familiar ones.
ISBN 0-06-008171-6 — ISBN 0-06-008172-4 (lib. bdg.)
1. Nursery rhymes. 2. Children's poetry. [1. Nursery rhymes.] I. Mother Goose. English. II. Title.
PZ8.3.E58 Mar 2005   2002151927
398.8—dc21   CIP
AC

Typography by Stephanie Bart-Horvath
9 10
❖
First Edition

for Mikayla!

the light of our lives

INTRODUCTION

Here are words both merry and wise. Mother Goose rhymes meet children at eye level with their colorful characters, disarming honesty, and playful feeling for life. Shunning pomposity and turning dull, predictable logic on its head, they miss nothing of sorrow or joy as they offer up words to caution the reckless, embolden the shy, encourage the adventurous, and give the youngest at bedtime the very thing they need: words of comfort, care, and love. How delightfully—and poetically—right it is that these strongly flavored, imagination-stretching rhymes should have come to be considered the work of an equally spry and fanciful author, a feathery personage as kindly and generous as the Tooth Fairy.

Fun to say and fun to hear, Mother Goose rhymes provide grown-ups with a welcome chance to set aside the day's cares and get silly with their children. There is no overstating the value of this, or the ease with which the rhymes allow and even encourage it to happen. Firm, infectious rhythms point the way, even for the hesitant newcomer to reading aloud:

Handy-spandy, Jacky dandy / Loves plum cake and sugar candy . . .

Rub-a-dub-dub, / Three men in a tub . . .

Lines as catchy as these are requested often, and soon learned by heart. And it is one of the happy truths about Mother Goose verses that it is absolutely impossible to sound *too* foolish while saying them. Passed down by word of mouth and through innumerable print editions for generations, these rhymes have proven to be among childhood's most durable playthings: brightly colored strings of words with the power to generate laughter and dreams.

Another reason for the rhymes' longevity has to do with all the useful bits of knowledge and worldly wisdom they encapsulate in the most enjoyable way possible. Better than any lesson is the Mother Goose rhyme about the lengths of the months, which begins, "Thirty days hath September. . . ." "Monday's child" does much the same for the days of the week. Other rhymes candidly illustrate the highs and lows that life may hold in store: the occasions when things don't go as planned (Poor Humpty Dumpty! Poor Jack and Jill!) as well as those when things go better than expected (just ask the very plum-y and pleased Little Jack Horner).

Some of the best-known rhymes shine a clarifying light on people—the classic *types* of people everyone meets up with eventually, whether in the sandbox or school yard or, a little while later, around the watercooler at work: dashing Bobby Shafto, lazy Little Boy Blue, merry Old King Cole. Proud Mrs. Hen, mother of ten. Clever, charm-drenched Terrence McDiddler, the "three-stringed fiddler." The foolhardy but incorrigible three wise men of Gotham. Better by far to experience strong, not always easily borne characters like these in Mother Goose before encountering them for real!

There is another way in which the rhymes help children to meet things as they are, head on. These days, the first rhymes most children know are those said or sung in television commercials. Against this backdrop, wise old Mother Goose holds out a refreshing, life-enhancing alternative: equally irresistible rhymes with nothing to sell. Children new to words need especially to experience inventive, memorable language uncluttered by salesmanship. They need to feel that the language they are just learning to speak, read, and write at home and in school is as much their own as anybody's. Mother Goose rhymes have the power to accomplish this because they represent language at its most playful and imaginative, and because they so clearly take the child's side.

In her wry and resoundingly good-natured illustrations, Mary Engelbreit takes the child's side too. The burnished ripeness of her artwork for this collection is a fine match for the spirit of the rhymes. For children, pictures as appealing as these come as a special kind of invitation. They serve as a gateway to the enjoyment of words on the page. And they usher children into a world worth knowing: the round, ripe Mother Goose world of pure possibility.

–Leonard S. Marcus
Author, critic, and children's literature historian

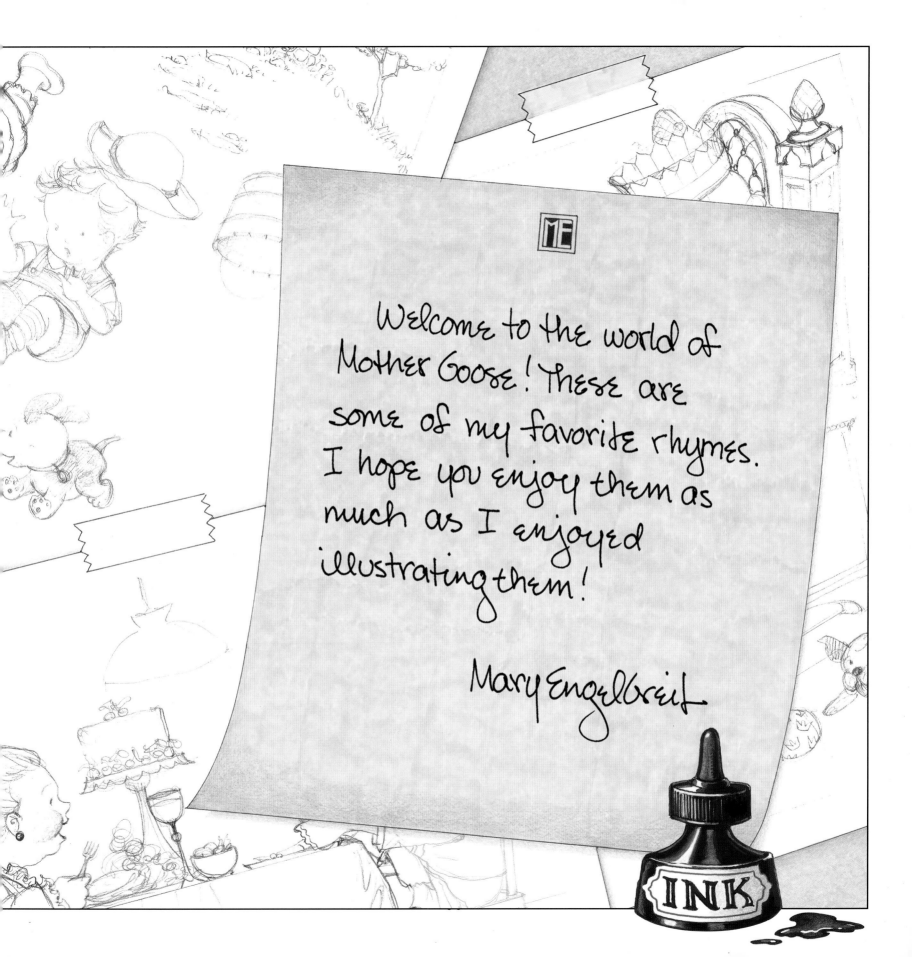

Welcome to the world of Mother Goose! These are some of my favorite rhymes. I hope you enjoy them as much as I enjoyed illustrating them!

Mary Engelbreit

Old Mother Goose,
When she wanted to wander,
Would ride through the air
On a very fine gander.

Little Bo-Peep has lost her sheep
And can't tell where to find them;
Leave them alone, and they'll come home,
Wagging their tails behind them.

Baa, baa, black sheep, have you any wool?

Yes, sir, yes, sir, three bags full.

One for my master, one for my dame,

And one for the little boy who lives down the lane.

I had a little nut tree,
Nothing would it bear
But a silver nutmeg
And a golden pear;
The King of Spain's daughter
Came to visit me,
And all for the sake
Of my little nut tree.

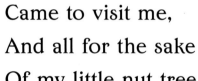

Handy-spandy, Jacky dandy,
Loves plum cake and sugar candy.
He bought some at the grocer's shop,
And pleased away went hop, hop, hop.

ittle Miss Muffet
Sat on a tuffet,
Eating her curds and whey;
Along came a spider,
Who sat down beside her
And frightened Miss Muffet away.

I love little kitty,
Her coat is so warm,
And if I don't hurt her
She'll do me no harm.
So I'll not pull her tail,
Nor drive her away,
But kitty and I
Very gently will play.
She shall sit by my side,
And I'll give her some food;
And kitty will love me
Because I am good.

Chook, chook, chook, chook, chook,
Good morning, Mrs. Hen.
How many chickens have you got?
Madam, I've got ten.
Four of them are yellow,
And four of them are brown,
And four of them are speckled red,
The nicest in the town.

Bat, bat,
Come under my hat,
And I'll give you a slice of bacon;
And when I bake,
I'll give you a cake
If I am not mistaken.

One leaf for fame,
One leaf for wealth,
One for a faithful lover,
And one leaf to bring glorious health,
Are all in a four-leaf clover.

Six little mice sat down to spin;
Kitty passed by and she peeped in.
What are you doing, my little men?
Weaving coats for gentlemen.
Shall I come in and cut off your threads?
No, no, Mistress Kitty, you'd bite off our heads.
Oh, no, I'll not;
I'll help you to spin.
That may be so,
But you can't come in.

Alittle pig found a fifty-dollar note,
And purchased a hat and a very fine coat,
With trousers, and stockings, and shoes,
Cravat, and shirt-collar, and gold-headed cane,
Then proud as could be, did he march up the lane;
Says he, "I shall hear all the news."

Mary had
a pretty bird,
Feathers bright
and yellow,
Slender legs—
upon my word
He was a
pretty fellow!

The sweetest note
he always sung,
Which much
delighted Mary.
She often, where
the cage was hung,
Sat hearing
her canary.

ack and Jill went up the hill
To fetch a pail of water;
Jack fell down and broke his crown,
And Jill came tumbling after.

Then up Jack got and off did trot,
As fast as he could caper,
To old Dame Dob, who patched his nob,
With vinegar and brown paper.

When Jacky's a good boy,
He shall have cakes and custard;
But when he does nothing but cry,
He shall have nothing but mustard.

Elsie Marley is grown so fine,
She won't get up to feed the swine,
But lies in bed till eight or nine.
Lazy Elsie Marley.

There was an old woman
Who lived in a shoe,
She had so many children
She didn't know what to do;
She gave them some broth
Without any bread;
She kissed them all soundly
And put them to bed.

29

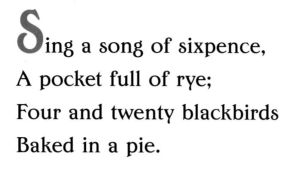

Sing a song of sixpence,
A pocket full of rye;
Four and twenty blackbirds
Baked in a pie.

When the pie was opened,
The birds began to sing;
Wasn't that a dainty dish
To set before a king?

The king was in his countinghouse,
Counting out his money;
The queen was in the parlor
Eating bread and honey.

The maid was in the garden,
Hanging out the clothes,
Along came a blackbird
And snapped off her nose.

Rub-a-dub-dub, three men in a tub,

And who do you think they be?

The butcher, the baker,

The candlestick-maker,

Turn them out, knaves all three.

The Queen
of Hearts,
She made
some tarts,
All on a
summer's day;
The Knave of Hearts,
He stole those tarts,
And took them
clean away.

The King of Hearts
Called for the tarts
And beat the knave full sore;
The Knave of Hearts
Brought back the tarts
And vowed he'd steal no more.

ack Sprat could eat no fat;

His wife could eat no lean;

And so betwixt them both, you see,

They licked the platter clean.

Old King Cole was a merry old soul
And a merry old soul was he;
He called for his pipe,
And he called for his bowl,
And he called for his fiddlers three.

Every fiddler, he had a fine fiddle,
And a very fine fiddle had he;
Oh, there's none so rare
As can compare
With King Cole
And his fiddlers three.

Three little ghostesses,
Sitting on postesses,
Eating buttered toastesses,
Greasing their fistesses,
Up to their wristesses,
Oh, what beastesses
To make such feastesses!

Pat-a-cake, pat-a-cake, baker's man!
Bake me a cake as fast as you can.
Roll it, and pat it, and mark it with B,
Put it in the oven for Baby and me.

Pussycat, pussycat,
Where have you been?
I've been to London
To look at the Queen.
Pussycat, pussycat,
What did you there?
I frightened a little mouse
Under her chair.

Oh where, oh where has my little dog gone?
Oh where, oh where can he be?
With his ears cut short and his tail cut long,
Oh where, oh where can he be?

Ride a cockhorse to Banbury Cross,
To see a fine lady upon a white horse;
Rings on her fingers and bells on her toes,
She shall have music wherever she goes.

Once I saw a little bird
Come hop, hop, hop;
So I cried, "Little bird,
Will you stop, stop, stop?"

I was going to the window
To say, "How do you do?"
But he shook his little tail,
And far away he flew.

Little King Pippin,
He built a fine hall,
Piecrust and pastry-crust,
That was the wall;
The windows were made
Of black pudding and white,
And slated with pancakes,
You ne'er saw the like.

This little piggie went to market,

This little piggie stayed at home,

This little piggie had roast beef,

This little piggie had none,

And this little piggie cried,

Wee-wee-wee-wee-wee,

All the way home.

Hot cross buns!
Hot cross buns!
One a penny, two a penny,
Hot cross buns!
If your daughters do not like them,
Give them to your sons;
But if you haven't any
of these pretty little elves
You can do no better than
eat them yourselves.

urly locks, curly locks,
Wilt thou be mine?
Thou shalt not wash dishes
Nor yet feed the swine;
But sit on a cushion
And sew a fine seam,
And feed upon strawberries,
Sugar and cream.

Ickle ockle, blue bockle,
Fishes in the sea,
If you want a pretty maid,
Please choose me.

Three young rats with black felt hats,

Three young ducks with white straw flats,

Three young dogs with curling tails,

Three young cats with demi-veils,

Went out to walk with two young pigs

In satin vests and sorrel wigs;

But suddenly

It chanced to rain

And so they all

Went home again.

Little lad, little lad,
Where were you born?
Far off in Lancashire,
Under a thorn,
Where they sup buttermilk
With a ram's horn;
And a pumpkin scooped,
With a yellow rim,
Is the bonny bowl
They breakfast in.

I had a little hen,
The prettiest ever seen;
She washed up the dishes,
And kept the house clean.

She went to the mill
To fetch me some flour,
And always got home
In less than an hour.

She baked me my bread,
She brewed me my ale,
She sat by the fire
And told a fine tale.

Humpty Dumpty sat on a wall,
Humpty Dumpty had a great fall.
All the king's horses
And all the king's men
Couldn't put Humpty Dumpty together again.

Three blind mice! See how they run!
They all ran after the farmer's wife.
She cut off their tails with a carving knife.
Have you ever seen such a sight in your life
As three blind mice?

There was a little boy went into a barn
And lay down on some hay;
An owl came out and flew about,
And the little boy ran away.

There was an old woman
Lived under a hill,
And if she's not gone
She lives there still.

To market, to market,
To buy a fat pig:
Home again, home again,
Jiggety jig.

The lion and the unicorn were fighting for the crown;
The lion beat the unicorn all around the town.
Some gave them white bread,
And some gave them brown;
Some gave them plum cake
And drummed them out of town.

Hickory, dickory, dock,
The mouse ran up the clock.
The clock struck one,
The mouse ran down,
Hickory, dickory, dock.

here was a little girl,
And she had a little curl
Right in the middle
Of her forehead;
When she was good
She was very very good,
But when she was bad
She was horrid.

What are little boys made of?
Frogs and snails
And puppy-dogs' tails,
That's what little boys
Are made of.

What are little girls made of?
Sugar and spice
And everything nice,
That's what little girls
Are made of.

Little girl, little girl,
Where have you been?
I've been to see Grandmother
Over the green.
What did she give you?
Milk in a can.
What did you say for it?
Thank you, Grandam.

Molly, my sister, and I fell out,
And what do you think it was all about?
She loved coffee and I loved tea,
And that was the reason we couldn't agree.

Dance, little Baby,
Dance up high!
Never mind, Baby,
Mother is by.
Crow and caper,
Caper and crow,
There, little Baby,
There you go!

Up to the ceiling,
Down to the ground,
Backwards and forwards,
Round and round;
Dance, little Baby,
And Mother will sing,
With the merry coral,
Ding, ding, ding!

Doctor Foster went to Gloucester
In a shower of rain;
He stepped in a puddle,
Right up to his middle,
And never went there again.

Rain on the green grass,
And rain on the tree,
Rain on the housetop,
But not on me.

If bees stay at home,
Rain will soon come;
If they fly away,
Fine will be the day.

The cock's on the rooftop
Blowing his horn,
The bull's in the barn
A-threshing the corn,
The maids in the meadow
Are making the hay,
The ducks in the river
Are swimming away.

Little boy blue,
Come blow your horn,
The sheep's in the meadow,
The cow's in the corn.
Where is the boy
Who looks after the sheep?
He's under a haystack
Fast asleep.

I saw a ship a-sailing,
A-sailing on the sea;
And, oh! It was all laden
With pretty things for thee!

There were comfits in the cabin
And apples in the hold;
The sails were made of silk,
And the masts were made of gold.

The four and twenty sailors
That stood between the decks
Were four and twenty white mice
With chains about their necks.

The captain was a duck,
With a packet on his back;
And when the ship began to move,
The captain said, "Quack! Quack!"

obby Shafto's gone to sea,
Silver buckles on his knee;
He'll come back and marry me,
Bonny Bobby Shafto!

Bobby Shafto's fat and fair,
Combing down his yellow hair;
He's my love forevermore,
Bonny Bobby Shafto!

Bobby Shafto's looking out,
All his ribbons flew about,
All the ladies gave a shout,
Hey for Bobby Shafto!

Ring around the rosies,
A pocket full of posies;
Ashes! Ashes!
We all fall down.

Here we go round the mulberry bush,
The mulberry bush, the mulberry bush,
Here we go round the mulberry bush,
So early in the morning.

Ring around the rosebush,
Three steps, four steps,
All the little boys and girls
Are sitting
On the doorsteps.

Three wise men of Gotham,
They went to Sea in a Bowl,
And if the Bowl had been stronger,
My Song had been longer.

Row, row, row your boat
Gently down the stream.
Merrily, merrily, merrily, merrily,
Life is but a dream.

istress Mary, quite contrary,
How does your garden grow?
With silver bells and cockle shells,
And pretty maids all in a row.

Thirty days hath September,
April, June, and November;
February has twenty-eight all alone,
All the rest have thirty-one,
Excepting leap year, that's the time
When February's days are twenty-nine.

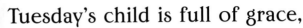Monday's child is fair of face,

Tuesday's child is full of grace,

Wednesday's child is full of woe,

Thursday's child has far to go,

Friday's child is loving and giving,

Saturday's child works hard for its living,

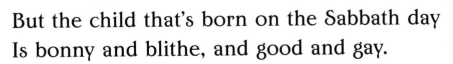But the child that's born on the Sabbath day
Is bonny and blithe, and good and gay.

The three little kittens
They lost their mittens,
And they began to cry,

Oh, Mother dear,
We sadly fear
Our mittens we have lost.

What? Lost your mittens,
You naughty kittens!
Then you shall have no pie.

Mee-ow, mee-ow, mee-ow.

No, you shall have no pie.

The three little kittens
They found their mittens,
And they began to cry,

Oh, Mother dear,
See here, see here,
Our mittens we have found.

Put on your mittens,
You silly kittens,
And you shall have some pie.

Purr-r, purr-r, purr-r,
Oh, let us have some pie.

Peter, Peter, pumpkin eater,
Had a wife and couldn't keep her.
He put her in a pumpkin shell
And there he kept her very well.

Little Jack Horner
Sat in a corner,
Eating his Christmas pie;
He put in his thumb,
And pulled out a plum,
And said, "What a good boy am I!"

There was a crooked man
Who walked a crooked mile.
He found a crooked sixpence
Against a crooked stile;
He bought a crooked cat,
Which caught a crooked mouse,
And they all lived together
In a little crooked house.

Simple Simon
Met a pieman
Going to the fair;
Says Simple Simon
To the pieman,
Let me taste your ware.

Says the pieman
To Simple Simon,
Show me first your penny;
Says Simple Simon
To the pieman,
Indeed I have not any.

A diller, a dollar,
A ten o'clock scholar,
What makes you
Come so soon?
You used to come
At ten o'clock,
But now you come
At noon.

Daffy-down-dilly
Is new come to town,
With a yellow petticoat
And a green gown.

Boys and girls come out to play,
The moon doth shine as bright as day.
Leave your supper and leave your sleep,
And join your playfellows in the street.
Come with a whoop and come with a call,
Come with a good will or not at all.
Up the ladder and down the wall,
A half-penny loaf will serve us all;
You find milk, and I'll find flour,
And we'll have a pudding in half an hour.

Diddle, diddle, dumpling, my son John
Went to bed with his stockings on;
One shoe off, and
one shoe on,
Diddle, diddle,
dumpling,
my son John.

Little Nancy Etticoat,
With a white petticoat,
And a red nose;
She has no feet or hands,
The longer she stands
The shorter she grows.

Jack be nimble,
Jack be quick,
Jack jump over
The candlestick.

ey diddle, diddle,
The Cat and the Fiddle,
The Cow jumped over the Moon,
The little Dog laughed
To see such sport,
And the Dish ran away
With the Spoon.

For want of a nail,
The shoe was lost;
For want of the shoe,
The horse was lost;
For want of the horse,
The rider was lost;
For want of the rider,
The battle was lost;
For want of the battle,
The kingdom was lost,
And all for the want
Of a horseshoe nail.

There came an old woman from France
Who taught grown-up children to dance;
But they were so stiff,
She sent them home in a sniff,
This sprightly old woman from France.

Lucy Locket lost her pocket,
Kitty Fisher found it;
Not a penny was there in it,
Only ribbon round it.

98

Little Poll Parrot sat in his garret
Eating toast and tea;
A little brown mouse jumped into the house
And stole it all away.

The north wind doth blow,
And we shall have snow,
And what will poor robin do then?
Poor thing.

He'll sit in a barn,
And keep himself warm,
And hide his head under his wing,
Poor thing.

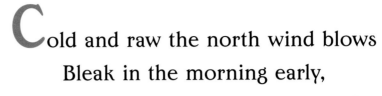

Cold and raw the north wind blows
Bleak in the morning early,
All the hills are covered with snow,
And the winter's now come fairly.

On the first of March
The crows begin to search;
By the first of April
They are sitting still;
By the first of May
They've all flown away,
Coming greedy back again
With October's wind and rain.

Hush a bye Baby
On the Tree Top,
When the wind blows
The Cradle will rock;
When the Bough breaks
The Cradle will fall,
And down will come Baby,
Cradle and all.

he Man in the Moon
Looked out of the moon,
Looked out of the moon and said,
"'Tis time for all children on the earth
To think about getting to bed!"

The rose is red, the violet's blue,
The honey's sweet, and so are you.
Thou art my love and I am thine;
I drew thee to my Valentine.
The lot was cast and then I drew,
And fortune said it should be you.

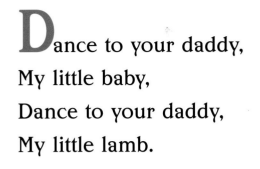

Dance to your daddy,
My little baby,
Dance to your daddy,
My little lamb.

You shall have a fishy
In a little dishy,
You shall have a fishy
When the boat comes in.

You shall have an apple,
You shall have a plum,
You shall have a rattle-basket
When your daddy comes home.

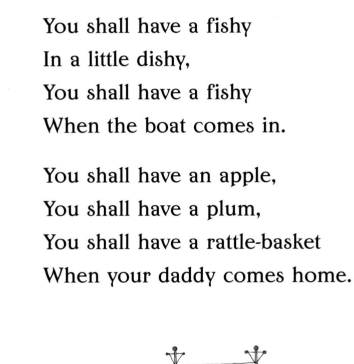

Rock-a-bye, baby,
Thy cradle is green,
Father's a nobleman,
Mother's a queen;
And Betty's a lady
And wears a gold ring;
And Johnny's a drummer
And drums for the king.

Hush, baby, my dolly,
I pray you don't cry,
And I'll give you some bread,
And some milk by-and-by;
Or perhaps you like custard,
Or maybe a tart,
Then to either you're welcome,
With all my heart.

Pease porridge hot,
Pease porridge cold,
Pease porridge in the pot,
Nine days old.
Some like it hot,
Some like it cold,
Some like it in the pot,
Nine days old.

Polly put the kettle on,
Polly put the kettle on,
Polly put the kettle on,
    We'll all have tea.

Sukey take it off again,
Sukey take it off again,
Sukey take it off again,
    They've all gone away.

Blow the fire and make the toast,
Put the muffins down to roast,
Blow the fire and make the toast,
    We'll all have tea.

Red sky at night,
Shepherd's delight;
Red sky in the morning,
Shepherd's warning.

Touch blue,
Your wish will come true.

Terrence McDiddler,
The three-stringed fiddler,
Can charm, if you please,
The fish from the seas.

Wee Willie Winkie
	Runs through the town,
Upstairs and downstairs
In his nightgown,
Rapping at the window,
Crying through the lock,
Are the children in their beds,
For now it's eight o'clock?

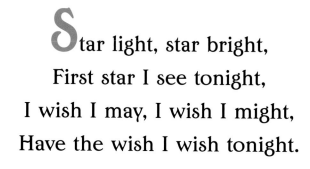

Star light, star bright,
First star I see tonight,
I wish I may, I wish I might,
Have the wish I wish tonight.

I see the moon,
And the moon sees me,
God bless the moon,
And God bless me.

Twinkle, twinkle, little star,
How I wonder what you are!
Up above the world so high,
Like a diamond in the sky.

Sleep, baby, sleep,
Our cottage vale is deep:
The little lamb is on the green,
With woolly fleece so soft and clean—
Sleep, baby, sleep.

Sleep, baby, sleep,
Down where the woodbines creep;
Be always like the lamb so mild,
A kind, and sweet, and gentle child.
Sleep, baby, sleep.

The cock crows in the morn
To tell us to rise,
And he that lies late
Will never be wise:
For early to bed,
And early to rise,
Is the way to be healthy
And wealthy and wise.

There was an old woman tossed up in a basket,
Seventeen times as high as the moon;
Where she was going I couldn't but ask it,
For in her hand she carried a broom.

Old woman, old woman, old woman, quoth I,
Where are you going to up so high?
To brush the cobwebs off the sky!
May I go with you? Aye, by-and-by.

A Note from Mary

When people ask what gave me the idea of illustrating a book of Mother Goose rhymes, I always think first of my granddaughter, Mikayla. Raising her has been an inspiration for me! I want my granddaughter to know the classic rhymes. Parents and grandparents are so tired of the commercialism of everything these days. These poems are innocent and bring children the enjoyment of simpler and slower times.

I also drew on my own childhood for inspiration. My clearest early memory of Mother Goose is my mother singing "Three Blind Mice," "Hickory Dickory Dock," and "Sing a Song of Sixpence" to me, so I'm very fond of these verses. I did have a Mother Goose book, but the pictures were dull and, frankly, I always was a little confused by it. Some of the rhymes don't really make sense when you listen to the words! When I created my own *Mother Goose*, I wanted to give the kids really great illustrations to help them enjoy the rhymes. And I wanted them to find plenty of things to look at in the pictures, so I've added lots of details.

I was thinking about Mikayla and other youngsters as I chose the poems for this

volume. HarperCollins asked the noted author and children's literature specialist Leonard S. Marcus to select about one hundred fifty of the rhymes for me to consider. I picked the ones that inspired a visual when I read them. I wanted to include the best-known rhymes, but also lesser-known ones that appealed to me.

To create each illustration, I read the poem and paid attention to the first image that jumped into my head. Actually I visualize the completed drawing before I ever start. It changes as I work on it, but usually I picture the final drawing first, and even "see" where the text will go a lot of times. I don't make a lot of "drafts" of my images—there's just one sketch, and it usually turns into the finished image, all on one piece of paper!

I drew "Little Miss Muffet" first. It was the one that most grabbed me. I wanted to draw that spider! And I wanted him to be a friendly-looking spider. The ship with twenty-four mice was the hardest, because I'd never drawn a ship before. I hope children have fun finding all twenty-four sailors—even the one in the hold. "The

Man in the Moon" was also difficult. I had to think a lot about how a man would look on the moon, but that picture turned out to be one of my favorites. Most of the drawings were easier, because the poems have so much in them. They give your imagination a place to start and so much to go on. My favorite is "Bat, Bat, Come Under My Hat." It makes absolutely no sense! And I also like "Three Little Ghostesses." It's really fun to say out loud.

Of course, all the rhymes are fun to read aloud. I'm always amazed at how quickly Mikayla memorizes the words! They have a rhythm that is easy to catch on to and repeat, which is really important for young children. And because they are so catchy and easy to remember, they've been around for a long time!

I hope that you will enjoy reading and sharing these classic poems. Be playful as you read. Try varying your voice. Let Mother Goose bring out the actor or actress in you! As you and your loved ones share these Mother Goose rhymes, I hope you'll find that they capture your heart as much as they have captured mine.

INDEX OF FIRST LINES